SHARE A STORY

TEN IN THE BED

Introduction

One of the best ways you can help
your children learn and learn to read
is to share books with them. Here's why:

• They get to know the **sounds**, **rhythms** and **words**
used in the way we write. This is different from how we
talk, so hearing stories helps children learn how to read.

• They think about the **feelings** of the characters
in the book. This helps them as they go about
their own lives with other people.

• They think about the **ideas** in the book. This helps
them to understand the world.

• Sharing books and listening to what your children
say about them shows your children that you care
about them, you care about what they think
and who they are.

Michael Rosen

Michael Rosen
Writer and Poet
Children's Laureate (2007-9)

For Brian and Daphne

First published 1988 by Walker Books Ltd
87 Vauxhall Walk, London SE11 5HJ

This edition published 2011

2 4 6 8 10 9 7 5 3 1

© 1988 Penny Dale
Concluding notes © CLPE 2011

The right of Penny Dale to be identified as author/illustrator of this work
has been asserted by her in accordance with the Copyright, Designs and Patents Act 1988

This book has been typeset in ITC Bookman Light

Printed in China

British Library Cataloguing in Publication Data:
a catalogue record for this book is available from the British Library

ISBN 978-1-4063-3494-4

www.walker.co.uk

TEN IN THE BED

Penny Dale

WALKER BOOKS
AND SUBSIDIARIES
LONDON · BOSTON · SYDNEY · AUCKLAND

There were ten in the bed and the little one said,
"Roll over, roll over!"

So they all rolled over and Hedgehog fell out ...
BUMP!

There were nine in the bed and the little one said,
"Roll over, roll over!"

So they all rolled over and Zebra fell out ...
OUCH!

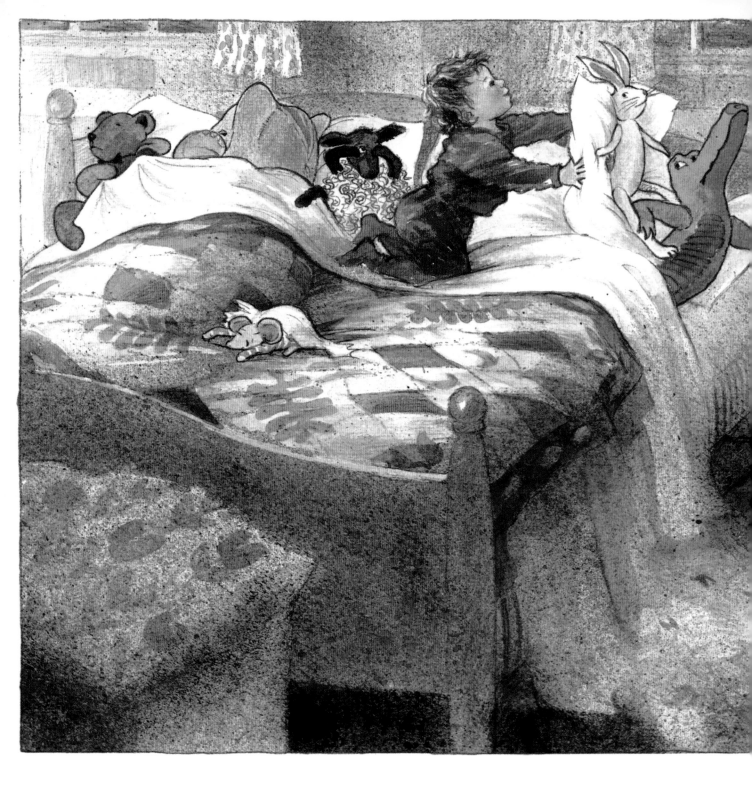

There were eight in the bed and the little one said,
"Roll over, roll over!"

So they all rolled over and Ted fell out ...
THUMP!

There were seven in the bed and the little one said,
"Roll over, roll over!"

So they all rolled over and Croc fell out ...
THUD!

There were six in the bed and the little one said,
"Roll over, roll over!"
So they all rolled over and Rabbit fell out ...
BONK!

There were five in the bed and the little one said,
"Roll over, roll over!"
So they all rolled over and Mouse fell out ...
DINK!

There were four in the bed and the little one said,
"Roll over, roll over!"

So they all rolled over and Nellie fell out ...
CRASH!

There were three in the bed and the little one said,
"Roll over, roll over!"

So they all rolled over and Bear fell out ...
SLAM!

There were two in the bed and the little one said,
"Roll over, roll over!"
So they all rolled over and Sheep fell out ...
DONK!

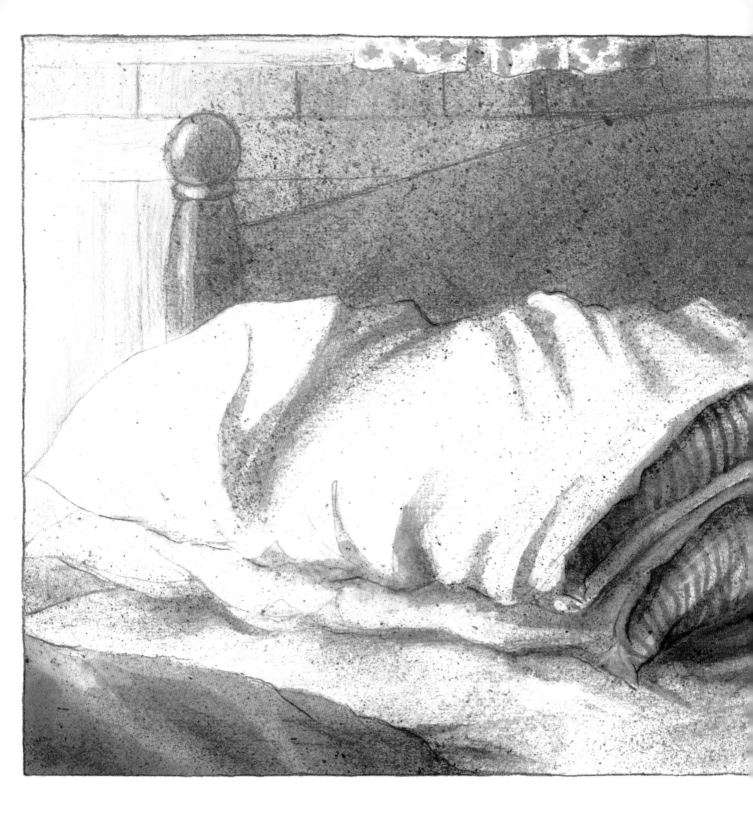

There was one in the bed and the little one said,

"I'm cold! I miss you!"

So they all came back and jumped into bed –
Hedgehog, Mouse, Nellie, Zebra, Ted,

the little one, Rabbit, Croc, Bear and Sheep.

Ten in the bed, all fast asleep.

Sharing Stories

Sharing stories together is a pleasurable way
to help children learn to read and enjoy books.
Reading stories aloud and encouraging children to
talk about the pictures and join in with parts of the
story they know well are good ways to build their
interest in books. They will want to share their favourite
books again and again. This is an important part
of becoming a successful reader.

Ten in the Bed is a memorable counting song which helps children to count from one to ten – and back again. Here are some ways you can share this book:

• The rhythm and rhyme are so strong in this book that children will know it well after a few readings. They will enjoy singing along, joining in with the words they remember and doing the actions for "Roll over, roll over".

• As each toy animal falls out of bed they land with a "thump", "ouch" or "crash"! Children can use their own toys to act out the story and shout out the different sounds as they land with a "bump" or a "thud" on the floor.

• When they know the story well, encourage children to tell it to you, using the pictures and turning the pages themselves.

• At the beginning of the story, children can hold up their ten fingers, folding one down each time a toy falls out of bed. As you read the rhyme, they can count them out and back into bed.

• What other counting rhymes and songs can you find? You can sing them together and act them out, using toys to add to the fun.

SHARE A STORY
A First Reading Programme
From Pre-school to School

Beginnings – 2 years+

Early Steps – 3 years+

Next Steps – 4 years+

Taking Off – 5 years+

Sharing the best books makes the best readers

WALKER BOOKS

www.walker.co.uk